BALTIMORE, A PARADISE

RAE SOWARDS

DEDICATED

To: You
From: Me

When I bow to you
I bow to the Universe
Inside of me and you
Within one action
A circle is being completed

"Sometimes you have to live on the edge to create the fear of falling, but know, there is no edge, only the Universe."

As she spoke those words, a small amount of blood dripped from her bottom lip; a branch must have hit her in the face during our escape. She stood upright, exposed to the damp air of the night and the awe-struck look upon my face. Her hair was wild and tangled, falling in chunky waves over her shoulders. Her body was toned, and small muscles framed her outline. Her stomach was strong and I could see each defined movement and contour with each deep breath she took. She had sweat covering her skin and it glowed the color of silver moonlight as if the moon were inside of her, bleeding out from every pore. She looked and I was gone, lost in her energy. I felt the love from her heart wrap around my single, lonely heart. I felt her hold me even though she stood several feet apart; she held my heart and at once she erased me. All the parts that I thought were my identity were gone. She birthed me that night, pushed me into a new way of believing in who I was, and showed me my place in the Universe.

For the first 17 years of my life, I believed I was Frances, born to Dale and Patricia in Baltimore in 1980. Those two thoughts alone were enough; they created a story, a certain set of circumstances that mapped out my life. Dale and Patricia were my parents, but they were also drug addicts, and because of this we had very little money. My mom, dad, and younger sister all lived in a small second-floor, one-bedroom apartment. From a young age, I was introduced to suffering and how survival was a desperate way to exist. Desperation could weaken the body and decompose the strongest of wills, but in some cases, this desperation could have the opposite effect. It could fortify the will of those who no longer wanted to suffer, and my story is about the latter.

In the beginning, my story was one filled with anger, sadness, and a disappointment I could not shake. Even in my happy moments, which were few, there was still a heaviness attached to me, a weight that reminded me this moment would pass. Happy moments would be interrupted by my mother stumbling in from a night out, high out of her mind, unable to make it up the stairs, or my father and his violent rages from my mother being out all night, in his words "doing God knows what." I knew what she was doing.

My mother would say, "Someone needs to support this family."

The night I met Jaana, she showed me I was so much more than Frances. What if I told you we are all so much more than our human identities? We are vast beings that have no birth and no death; we have existed since the beginning and have played every part here on Earth and it is our job to know this and wake from the dream.

I first met Jaana in 1997. I had just turned 17 years old; it was at the end of my senior year. The night we met was my senior prom. A prom I did not go to. The ticket for the prom was over fifty dollars, which I didn't have. Plus, that aside, I did not have anyone to go with—not a single friend, let alone a date. From the earliest time I could remember, I had always been somewhat of a loner.

On the night I met Jaana, I took a walk. I left my house around 8:00 pm. The prom started at 8:30 pm, and I started to walk downtown toward the hotel where it was being held. I wanted to take a look and get a glimpse from afar. That way if someone ever asked, "Did you go to prom?" I could say, "Well, yeah, sort of." Plus I needed a walk and it was an excuse for a destination.

As I walked, I looked up at the night sky, deep into its infinity. The sky was a milky haze, thick and black, the darkest of mud. It hung heavy and low with humidity. I thought if I reached up I could stir the night to sleep with my fingertips. These nights were common for

Baltimore in late June. A thunderstorm would have been a nice reprieve from the heat of the day that had turned into the heat of the night. On that night, I walked the streets to find a breeze, hidden behind an alleyway or an underpass. Anything to rid me of my family's despair. My dad sat passed out on the sofa from a handful of pills he had taken an hour earlier. My mother was out trying to score some more pills for tomorrow. She would soon be next to my father—passed out together in a dream of forgetfulness. I envied how they could escape it all in sleep. I had always stayed away from drugs. I saw how drugs had ruined both my parents' lives and I didn't want to go down that path as well. Oh, but to forget it all at will whenever you wanted sounded nice.

My younger sister Heather was over at a friend's house to spend the night. Heather had the ability to disappear from the eternal struggle that was our childhood home. Unlike me, Heather was popular. Just the night before, she entered the house smoking a Newport 100, stolen from our mom's purse. She had a new boyfriend with her. A tall, skinny white kid with bad acne. He was wearing a Wu-Tang shirt and a backward Orioles cap. Both did not say a word to me as they ran straight to the kitchen, grabbed our half-empty two-liter of Pepsi and a bag of UTZ chips, rushed past me with food in hand, and out the door again. Heather was three years younger than me and had had a handful of boyfriends already. I, on the other hand… I had not had one date, let alone a boyfriend. I wasn't really interested in boys. Girls had always held my interest more. However, declaring myself a lesbian and dating women was not something I was ready for. My life seemed complicated enough.

Solitude became my friend. I didn't mind it most days. I would lose myself in thoughts. Other days it was harder to bear. I would call it the loneliness—it never lasted long, but when it hit, it was like a truck hitting a brick wall. It was a hurt that is hard to describe. If you have experienced it, then you know. I do not have to explain. It was as if my heart ached for someone out in the void, someone I didn't even know to soothe the hurt inside of me.

My walks were the closest to escape I had. I felt it was the only time I had some control over my life while at the same time giving up control. I allowed the Universe to direct my walks, taking me where my intuition directed me.

Each step on my walk took me deeper into the city, deeper into my head, farther away from the loneliness, and deeper into myself.

Then I would be reminded of where I was. The smell of urine from the alleyways. The rotting fish and the salt from the brackish water of the inner harbor all mixed in the air and absorbed into my skin.

The environment and my body became so entangled that I swear I could have dissolved into a thousand pieces if only the wind blew from the right direction, scattering the cells of my body into the dark night. No one would know I was gone; no evidence to collect to say I was ever here. On some nights, I wished for this more than anything—to have it all disappear. I wanted the loneliness and the sadness to go, but because I was stubborn, I'd say fuck it, make all of my life disappear. On the night I met Jaana, this feeling was at its height.

My stomach growled as I neared the hotel.

I turned the corner onto Boston Street. A circus of eateries, mostly sub shops and Chinese takeout stores, lined up in a row, their yellow light in the purple darkness of the night calling me in like a moth to the flame. The smell always made my stomach ache for a taste, but more often than not, I didn't have enough money for even a fortune cookie. That night was no different: no money and no food.

I turned the corner off the busy street into an alleyway with only two street lights, one of which was busted out. The broken glass crunched beneath my feet. It must have just happened. It was dark. I could only see a few feet in front of me. I often took this way. It was a shortcut to the water, but tonight it was darker than the other nights because of the broken street light. The shortcut would save me a good fifteen minutes and I was already five minutes in, so I walked on. The rats were in a fever tonight; they ran across my feet. I walked loud to scare them off. One approached and stood directly in front of me, cocking its head as if it were a dog and wanted to play. I bent down to put my hand out but at the last minute, I jerked back. I could feel the rats bumping into the back of my heels, and when the rats were not at my heels, I would hear the occasional pop of a water bug from underneath my feet. I didn't mean to step on them. The whole alley was full of their black, hard-shelled bodies. At times, the black asphalt looked as if it were moving from the amount of water bugs clustered together in the alley that night.

In the familiar noise of the city, which makes its own quiet, there was a new noise, a different noise, like a panting from a dog. I turned to listen, titling my head, squinting to make out the noise. But as soon as I repositioned my body in the direction of the sound, it stopped.

I froze, still, my hand in a tight fist. I shook my head to clear the moment and listened again. Nothing.

"Hey, I can see you," I said out loud. "Come out." My voice echoed through the alleyway. I yelled in my most assertive voice with only the tiniest of a tremble at the bottom of my throat. I hoped they could not hear my fear.

Behind a dark outline of what looked to be trash cans, I saw a pointed ear from what looked like a dog. I thought it might be one of the pit bulls used for dog fights; maybe it had escaped. I pulled out my pocket knife slowly and quietly opened it. I had no intention of hurting the dog, but I wanted to be prepared if it attacked without warning. I held the knife tightly in my hand, my hand numbing as all the blood rushed from my fingers.

I remember the night my mother gave me the knife. It was on my 13th birthday. I had just finished eating crabs, my father's birthday present to me. Each year since I was eight he had given me the same thing for my birthday, a dozen medium female crabs. My father would say with a wink, "The females are sweeter," and then he would smile wide, his two front teeth missing.

After eating the crabs, I scrubbed my hands with lemon juice to remove the smell, causing a slight sting. I had several small cuts on my hands left from the claws of the crabs as I picked them apart to eat. Their last attempt to defend themselves, for even in death they still had the desire to live, I thought.

As I walked from the kitchen, my mother grabbed my arm and turned me around so we were face to face. We were almost the same height.

My mother said with a nervous laugh, "If you're going to walk the streets all night, you have to be able to take care of yourself. I don't want to find out you were robbed or worse."

I thought of all the things that could be worse. I knew what they were and it frightened me too. I looked down at my feet, looking past the small-framed figure that was my mother. Her face looked even older than the day before. But always the same eyes, two small, wrinkled slits simmering with a soft sadness that I would never fully understand. Her face transformed in front of me, her eyes becoming narrow.

She said, "Goddamn it, Frances, be careful out there." She took a long drag of her cigarette, paused for the inhale, then said with the exhale, "Fuck, I love you kid" in one breath, then placed her hand on my cheek, directing my face out of the path of the smoke. There are so many small ways people show their love when they have so little to give.

She was done with the conversation. Her right arm brushing against my arm, creating a slight breeze, I inhaled the familiar scent. Alcohol, vanilla, and cigarettes. I watched my mom walk out the door and into the night; into her own uncertainty. I hoped she had taken her knife as well because I worried, too.

I knew my mother didn't have much to give and I did not want to push her, afraid she would give too much and disappear into the night forever.

Now, I gripped the knife and turned and walked fast toward the end of the alley. I reached the end of the alley and arrived at a busy city street. The harbor was in sight. A giant black pool of still water reflecting a mirror image of a city turned upside down. Benches all along the waterfront lined the water's edge. In the middle of the day, white-collar downtown city men and women ate their lunches in the sun on those benches.

At night, however, the benches belonged to the other half. The homeless used the benches for beds. The teenagers used it as a place to gather and be someplace, any place other than home. Just like me, most lived in their own broken-down families, looking for an escape from the heat on this summer night.

One of the boys, a large white kid with a buzz cut, walked past me and bumped hard into my left shoulder. As I walked by, he said under his breath, "Hey nigger, are you a girl or a boy?" Then he laughed to himself and stumbled away, throwing his skateboard hard to the cement, pushing off even harder past me, laughing the whole way.

I was called that name a lot, the N- word. I had been called it so often in my 17 years of life that it no longer fazed me like it did when I was younger. It did sting a little when the word first hit; like a slap to the face, only the first few seconds stung, but I was able to shake it off like a dog shakes off any hurt that it's subjected to. But it always hurt less when it came from a stranger. However, when people in my family called me the N-word, now that was a hurt that I carried. I would probably carry it for the rest of my life. I had not learned to shake it off.

I was the only black person in my family. My mother, father, and sister were all white. My white mother had me after four years of marriage to my white father. How did she birth a half black baby? She never talked about it. In fact, no one in my family talked about it. However, I still continued to exist.

The thing is I rarely thought about it. Maybe because that was how it had always been. I'd never known a different life. It is funny the things we think are normal; the things we become used to. My family who raised me, "loved me," fed me, clothed me, but never accepted me. On occasion, my mother and father would put me in my place by calling me the N- word when I was misbehaving. In their minds, it was a way to show they were just a little better than me because they were born white.

I found an empty bench close enough to the water. Across the pier, I could see the hotel where the prom was taking place. I could see the lights and hear the music. It was so close but in my mind so far from me and my life. It was as if in another reality, one I could only see but not be a part of.

I sat on the bench by the water, close enough to see my reflection in the black pool of shit water from the harbor. It smelled of dead fish. The smell reminded me of my situation. A situation in which I was lost. Comforted by my sadness, I wore it in the heat of the night, wrapping it willingly and intentionally all around me, placing most of its weight on my back. I knew I couldn't carry it any longer, and before I cut it out of me I wanted to feel all of its weight—its suffocating heaviness—one more time. I wanted to mourn its passing. I was tired of pretending it wasn't there and tired of not allowing myself to feel its weight pressing into every part of my body.

For the first time, I cried; I sobbed like a dying person.

Tears streamed down my face. I cried for my mother to comfort me but I knew she did not even know how to comfort herself. My tears landed in the murky waters of the harbor.

The salt from my tears cut through the thick black oil in the water.

Then, through one of the ripples created by my tear, I saw through the black of the water and it was clear. For a second I thought I could see to the bottom. It was crystal blue. I saw fish, and not the rotten ones floating on top, but deep beneath the water they were swimming and were vibrant in color and I swear they had smiles on their faces. I could see the sandy bottom, a white sand that sparkled silver and gold flakes. I blinked. I did not believe what I was seeing.

A hidden paradise right beneath my feet?

No, this was only a mirage. Just like a person dying of thirst seeing water in the desert. I was seeing a paradise in Baltimore.

"A paradise in Baltimore," I said out loud with a snicker. *I must be dying.* I heard hallucinations were common right before the end.

Just then I heard a man shout, "Hey kid!"

The man stood behind me yelling in my ear. "Hey kid, get the fuck off of my bench."

I froze in fear; something in his voice sounded terrifying.

"I'm leaving," I said.

"What did you just say?" The man stood close; his breath smelled heavily of alcohol. He grabbed my face, squeezing my cheeks together. At first, I was nervous he would feel the wetness from my tears. I did not want him to know that I was crying. Then I realized he was not letting go, only squeezing harder and more violently. I tried pushing him away, but he was a big man, and I was only five feet two inches tall. I kicked him in the knee and he let go. I ran but he grabbed me by the back of the shirt and surrounded me with his whole body, closing his arms tight around my waist. His hand moved upward, rubbing up against my chest, grabbing my small breasts, squeezing them the same way he squeezed my face, like it was his; like it had always been his. His breathing was heavy. The spit from his thick breath mixed with the humidity in the air. My tears were now salty bricks, their weight pulled me deeper into the hell of the moment

I remembered my knife. I tried to free my hands, but he was holding them too tight.

I froze. I closed my eyes. I told myself I could leave my body now if I wanted to.

I no longer felt the pressure of his arms around my body like a straightjacket. I only felt his arm brush mine as he ran past me toward the east end of the city.

I stood still, breathing heavily, my body shaking from adrenaline. Sweat ran down my face, and as the wind blew I felt a slight coolness come over my burning body. I fell to the ground, and as I fell, my head shifted to the right. and out of the corner of my eye: a dog? A big dog, the biggest dog I had ever seen, more like a wolf than a dog. Its enormous body was a beautiful and terrifying sight. Its large light brown eyes looked human, and they looked right at me. They looked at me with such love and know-ingness. I never wanted them to stop looking. I needed to know what this look meant. At once, I had no fear. I stood still and I did not want to scare it. But I knew this living thing would never hurt me. It was here to protect me. It approached first, placing one paw out slowly but steadily, a low muffle releasing from its throat and its head nodding up and down as it walked toward me.

And that was when I knew it was a girl. The way she stood over top of me was like how a mother stands over her pups when danger is approaching. I put my hand out so she could smell me, and she licked my hand. I stood slowly and turned my legs in the direction of home. We walked side by side for a while. I was still shaken. An older man walked past us, and before I had a chance to jump in fear from the approaching footsteps. The dog could sense it and she rubbed her strong back against the outside of my right leg.

Just then, I exhaled the breath I had been holding in since the horrible event took place. The haze from the heat broke and the sky opened, and for the first time that night I saw the moon. It was bright and it illuminated the darkness. It was the fullest moon I had ever seen and the light from it turned the dog's black fur a shade of deep midnight blue.

I finally arrived home. To say goodbye, I turned and bent down on one knee. We were now face to face, and those light brown eyes again looked right into mine. I swear I could see into another world. They looked at me as if they had known me forever, as if they loved me with certainty. They looked at me as if nothing bad had ever happened to me, as if I were innocent and deserving of all the love in the Universe. I hugged her warm fur body. She turned and walked away. I was about to go into the apartment, but I had to know more. Who was behind those eyes?

I followed her. To see where she had come from. To see where she was going. I ran toward the alleyway, where she had just turned the corner. I arrived and saw a whirling blue light in the shape of an oval. It had tiny white lines moving in a round motion, and within the lines were tiny triangles in all directions that swirled in unison. It looked like a portal of energy. At first, I was nervous and unsure. But whatever part of me connected to those eyes overpowered any fear I had and I jumped through the light. Placing my hands out, I protected my face, afraid I would end up plowing into the brick building that was behind the light.

With my eyes closed and my hands in guard, I jumped. At once I was pulled upward, my body spinning with the motion of being sucked up. It felt dizzying. I opened my eyes. The blue light was still there. Then there was darkness, and my body came to a heavy stop. I fell what seemed like only a few feet, my butt hitting the ground first. I was unsure where I was. It was still dark. I placed my hands next to the bottom of my thighs to feel what I was sitting on. It felt like grass—smooth, cool grass. However, as I ran my fingertips over the grass, I could feel a vibration, a tinkle in the grass as if it were alive. I jumped up to my feet, and with that, the darkness turned into sunrise and within seconds the area was illuminated with the early morning light you see at first break. A soft, blue light, aching to be touched. I put my hands out, trying to catch the blue in the hush of the mist, but each attempt evaded me. I knew it could never be claimed or be caught.

I widened my eyes to take a full look around. I was standing in an open field in the blue light of dawn. To the right there was a patch of wildflowers and a small creek. Before me I saw a field of grass in the distance and there was a forest line maybe a mile away. I stood in an open field. I could hear a humming in the background. From birds or insects? There was a stillness to this place that captivated all of me. I could smell the sweetness in the wildflowers. I could taste mint from the pine trees that were far in the distance. I could feel the vibration of the grass beneath my feet. I found it strange that I knew instinctively where each taste, smell, and touch came from. I knew the very source. I knew that this was nature in its purest form..

"Frances, Frances," a small voice said from behind me.

I turned and a young woman who looked to be in her early twenties walked toward me. She knew my name and she repeated it.

"What are you doing here?" she asked.

I started walking backwards away from her, but still facing her. I said, "I don't know. I don't know. Where am I?"

The woman replied, "You followed me through the blue light? "

"Those wolf 's eyes," I said. "I had never seen eyes filled with so much love. I had to know."

"You were not supposed to follow me," she said.

I said, "You… you are the wolf?"

"Yes, I was the wolf, but now I am human. You can call me Jaana. Frances, we have to get you home, it is not your time to be here."

I moved in close to Jaana, looking into her eyes, seeing if she really was the wolf that saved my life. The eyes were a different color from the light brown they were before, now a much deeper brown, richer, and for a second I thought she was lying. Those eyes were not the same. Then, in that same thought, they changed not color but intent, and all the love came rushing through her eyes again right into my heart. I knew she was the wolf—the same being in two forms.

Jaana reached down slowly for my hand, placing hers in mine. When her hand touched me, it felt like a memory of knowingness. A memory I did not know that I had forgotten. Her thin hand seemed to merge into mine as if her hand slipped underneath the skin of my own hand, finding a home between the flesh and bone, never to leave once inside.

"Follow me," she said in a low voice.

We started walking toward the forest line. After a little time, she stopped and said, "The portal is closed now. We have to find a new portal that will get you home." For the first time, her calm demeanor changed. She seemed rushed, uncertain what to do next.

"Are you okay?" I said, concerned.

"I am okay, Frances. It is just that we have to get you back to Earth or your timeline may be changed forever. Sorry, I am feeling a little out of sorts. It is because Earth's vibration is still running through me."

She stopped walking, stood in front of me, and said, "I don't have to tell you this, Frances, I know you already know. Earth is a hard place to live. It has many obstacles that keep a consciousness from seeing its true self. I know this and still I am responding to its effects on me. Now I have more understanding for those consciousnesses who choose to live on Earth."

"Choose to live there?" I asked. "Is it a choice? Why would I choose to live on Earth? Like you said, it is hard and complicated. Are there easier planets to exist on?" I asked.

"Yes, a lot are easier, and in truth there are more difficult ones too. We don't call them planets here, but realities. When you use the word 'planets,' it makes you think of something fixed, heavy, and dense, but in truth nothing is made of physical matter. A planet just appears to be physical. In truth, Earth and other realities like it are made up of information and data, and data is fluid, changeable, and constantly able to be more than what it appears to be. There are realties with no war, no hate, and no injustices. They don't even have a name for it. They exist perfectly in harmony and love."

"Then why would a consciousness, as you call them, choose to live on Earth?"

"Because, Frances, Earth is where you learn the most and are tested on who you really are, what is most im-portant to who you are, and what your soul's purpose is. On Earth, every day you must make a choice between fear and love. Many beings choose Earth because it is a fast track to enlightenment and really one of the only places to attain enlightenment."

"Enlightenment, what is that? I have an idea of what it is, but it might not be what I think."

Jaana answered, "Enlightenment is when the Universe source reveals to you your true nature and who you really are, and then a door is opened. You are allowed to enter into a new and different reality where you are a part of everything and a part of nothing at the same time. Because you are a part of everything, there is no separation, and because there is no separation, everything is you. You can love everything in the same way you love yourself, but without ego, which means unconditional love. When you love everything un-conditionally, you now love like the Source loves, and be-cause of that you are allowed in on the cosmic dream."

"The cosmic dream?" I asked. "What is that?"

"All of these realities, including Earth, are all a dream. I need to explain this more…"

Jaana looked at me, her concern now gone. A calm-ness came over her.

"I know," said Jaana. "Let's Meditate. This will raise my vibration and the answers will come to me about how to get you back home. Sit with me, Frances. We need to meditate. Let's ask the Universe what the next step in the chapter is."

We sat cross-legged in some sort of pretzel shape. She showed me the correct position.

"Do you feel comfortable?" Jaana asked. I said I did, but I did not. It had only been a few minutes and my legs were already cramping. However, cramping legs seemed like the least of my worries, so I did not argue.

"Okay, let everything go. Clear the mind. If a thought comes in, let it pass, acknowledge it, but then let it fly by out the window of your mind. Breathe in and out of your nose and focus on the sensation of the inhale and exhale through the nostrils. Can you feel the slight air right underneath the nostrils on your upper lip?" Jaana asked.

"Yes," I said.

"What does it feel like?" she asked.

"A slight tingle," I said.

"What else do you feel, Frances?"

"The inhale is cool and the exhale is warm."

"Yes, very, very good. Focus on all the sensations of the breaths in and out of the nose. It is very important."

Within a few moments of silence, I started to see swirling colors, first yellow, then it changed into a deep, dark purple. The color looked like an ink blot of light that moved up and down and side to side behind my eyes. It moved like the liquid in a lava lamp, fluid and without hesitation. It put me into a trance. At once a forest appeared again from behind the backs of my eyes. It was as if a small movie were playing only for me. An image of the forest appeared; it was rich with pine trees shown as a silhouette above me as if I were lying on the forest floor, looking up into the night sky. Then, from out of the corner of my eye the moon slowly rolled into the scene. I could see it through the smoky haze of the night clouds. Oh, but the full moon was illuminated with such intensity I could see every crater every bump of its rocky surface.

The image was beautiful and it relaxed me. I had a feeling this vision was more than a vision but a place that I belonged. With that, the image faded and Jaana said softly, "I know where we have to go. I know the exact location of an open portal. It will only be open for a short time; we must go now."

We walked what seemed like all day. Only a few words were spoken between us. I was still in shock and Jaana seemed like she needed time to think.

Several hours passed. The sun was setting a yellow-orange reflected off of the grass, the flowers, the bark of the tree. The trees grew more in number as we walked into what seemed to be a dense forest. The birds stopped their songs as the slow night rolled in.

Jaana, sensing my apprehension of the approaching night, looked over and said, "Frances, We are going to do this together, I've got you!" Then she smiled, the yellow sunset becoming a dark orange hue against her face.

"We will be approaching the path that leads to where the portal is," she continued. "The portal will be guarded by Nogos. Once on that path, we must be extremely quiet because they have a keen sense of hearing. We should take our shoes off."

"Nogos, what are Nogos?" I said.

"They are beings that protect the portals. It is very dangerous to travel through portals without permission from the higher beings. I had to ask permission to go through the portal to go to Earth to save your life. I knew the man by the bench would attack you and that it would not end well. He was going to hurt you. I had seen it in a vision and I knew it was not your time to die.

"That was going to be your fate. I first tried to stop you by having the street light go out. I know you have a fear of the dark and I thought this might make you turn around and take a longer route to the harbor, making you miss bumping into the man by a couple of seconds. Sometimes it takes just a few seconds to change the course of a life. But you and your stubbornness and your desire to always go against what is easier is something I love about you. However at that moment it really frustrated me," she said as she bumped into my shoulder with a grin on her face. "See, I was watching you the entire time. This is when I knew I would have to ask for permission to leave and come to Earth in my wolf form to save you.

"Back to the Nogos, they are beings that protect the portals so us higher and lower beings do not enter Earth and change people's destinies by entering realities we do not have permission to use and venture into.

"Higher beings and lower beings?" I asked.

"Yes, Nogos are found in all realities. There are realities that are made up of all higher beings, also known as loving beings. The reality we are in now is like this. All the beings here love unconditionally. However, there are realities that are made up of all negative beings that want to bring chaos and destruction."

I asked, "Is that what Earth is?"

"No," said Jaana. "Earth is special because it has both higher and lower beings. That is why Earth is so important. It is a place where the Universe balances itself. Earth is used as a gauge, like an ongoing self-evaluation for God to see themselves. Earth is like God's barometer. To see how and where they can improve. God is improving. Yes, they are evolving, becoming just like us because we are them. God is extremely more evolved than us, but our evolution is tied to theirs."

I asked, "Are there many Gods?"

"Yes, but the God I am speaking of, there is just one. I call God 'they' because God is not he or she. God is a being with no gender. We could replace the word God with 'Source.' Let's do that. It will make it easier for everyone. Let's call them Source."

"What is the Source's goal? What do they want the final results to be?" I asked.

"'Final results' sounds like a very human phrase. There is no final result; evolution continues on and on there is always room to evolve. But I can see you want an answer. The uncomplicated answer would be love. Source wants everyone to love each other."

"Love… love is not a simple thing," I said. "I know people who have said they love me and then they hurt me. I don't think love will fix this."

Jaana replied, "Not love, but unconditional love. The love that made you follow me into the portal. That was your first experience with unconditional love. It is a love that only gives; it never takes. It is never in need; it has no expectations. It does not judge; it only wants freedom for all beings. Source wants you to love like the way they love you, unconditionally."

With a serious but peaceful look on her face, Jaana paused and spoke, as if she were reciting something.

"Every day, God wipes us clean
To love someone so much
That you give them a will
That is based on freedom
God loves
Like a mountain built on the edge of a cliff
Unafraid to fall."

"Wait, I thought we were calling God 'Source,'" I said.

"Yes, thank you, Frances. I forgot. It is just one of my poems, and in the poem I used the word 'God.' It was before we decided to change God to Source."

"Oh, like when we decided two minutes ago to do that?" I joked.

"Exactly, Frances," Jaana said with a laugh. "Let me continue, Frances, unless you believe we cannot finish without an important discussion on God and Source and which to use when."

"No, no," I said. "Please continue." I made a circle gesture with my right hand to motion her to continue.

She laughed again, but this time harder.

"The transformation into unconditional love can only happen one being at a time. But if enough beings evolve in the same reality around the same time, it can make it easier for all beings in that reality to rise up and increase their ability to become love, changing that reality, lifting it to a higher consciousness level," Jaana said. "I am a higher being. I once was in human form. I have lived on Earth and other realities like Earth. I have had many lives, too many to count, over hundreds of thousands. I finally advanced to this state. I no longer have to go back to Earth unless I choose to go back. Most evolved beings do choose to go back. We return to teach, mostly to be an example of a being that can love unconditionally. We have great empathy for them because we have been where they are. It might have been thousands of years ago, but we remember the struggle and want to lend our wisdom to the cause.

"This reminds me about the Nogos. They were created solely to protect the portals. However, after many lives, the Nogos can evolve into higher beings. This is based on the eighth law of the Universe, which states perpetual transmutation of energy."

"What does that mean?"

Jaana said in a clear voice, like reciting the law from a book she had filed in a top-secret place only she was allowed to see, "It states that all beings have within them the power to change the conditions in their lives. Higher vibrations consume and transform lower ones. Thus, each of us can change the energies in our lives by understanding the Universal Laws and applying the principles in such a way as to effect change."

I said with a puzzled look on my face, "Anyone can change their life and make it better?"

"Yes," said Jaana.

"Can you make someone love you? Can you make a parent love you more?"

"Well, no," said Jaana.

"Then I don't believe what you are saying is true. How can a person have a better life if they never get the love they so desperately need?"

"First, let me say Frances, love is not a need. If you need love from someone, then it is not real love, it is desire. You can never make someone change or try to get them to do something they do not want to do. They have to want to do it of their own free will and have a true intent to do it. It has to come from their heart, not their mind. However, there *is* a way for the child, the person you speak of, to find happiness and the love they feel they are missing."

"How?" I said, my eyes open, waiting for her knowledge to spill into me.

"They find the love they are missing inside of them. They need to go on a quest inward to meet their higher self where all the love of the Universe sits waiting for them. They must gently knock on the door and ask to come in. The smaller self has to meet the higher self in the middle. There is a point in the Universe, right in the middle, where time and space disappear and the smaller self finds an opening in time, a door. When the higher self, also known as the eternal self, meets the personal self, also known as the ego self, this is when the personal self sees who they really are, and all the love they have been searching for in other people, material things, and status is revealed to them. They understand that love can only come from the higher self because it is the source of who they are. And no one, no outside object will give them the deep sense of love like their own true self can. Do you understand, Frances?"

"Yes, I think so," I said. "I know people have said you have to love yourself first before you can love anyone else. I have also heard money does not buy love. I guess this is where the sayings are coming from. The part I think I do not understand is how do I truly love myself when I am lacking all of the things I so desperately need to make my life better?"

"Yes," said Jaana. "People do not fully understand. They have a misunderstanding of what love is. They look for love in their personal-ego self, but the ego self cannot love; it is an illusion. The ego self does not really exist; it has no real substance. The human being needs to go past the personal ego self to the higher self—the self with no form, no body, no personality, no identity. The self that has nothing to lose because it already has everything it needs. It is complete and full; it is enough."

"How do you start such a quest? How do you find the eternal self? You say the eternal self has no name, no identity, no form. How do you call out for someone with no name?" I asked.

Jaana said, "You call out in desperation. With the thoughts, *I want to know more. I want to be more. I want to be better.* Behind desperation is love. Love for what is missing; love for who and what you truly are. Just call out.

"Once the call is made, the higher self will come. With your true intention to know the truth, the higher self will come. You cannot merely speak the words, 'I want to know.' You have to feel it at the being level. This will get the attention of the eternal self and it will run to you the way a mother runs to her child when it is lost and is in need. You have to call out like you are in need, because in fact, you are. Most people are. The problem is they don't know it. Rather, they *do* know it but they think material things and other people will fill that need. They have no idea what the higher self is, let alone that it is the thing they long for the most in this world.

"After the call is made, the next step is forgiveness. The eternal self will help the ego self. She will give love, insight, wisdom, and the strength to forgive. Forgiveness takes great strength and courage because it removes a guard one thinks is necessary to exist in this world. But again, this world is not real and that guard is an illusion. Forgiveness is unconditional love, which is your true state. You are removing the false to see the truth."

Then Jaana paused again and recited,

*"Familiarize yourself with the false
For that is where the truth can be found
For what is real can never be hidden
Not even in the false"*

I looked down and said nothing.

My mind still caught in her teaching, I whispered, "Not even in the false can truth hide."

I looked up and then I saw it! The place from behind my eyes when I was meditating. It was exactly the same. The silhouette of the tree, the moon, rolling clouds— even the feeling of home hit me again. "Déjà vu," I whispered to myself.

"Take your shoes off!"

"What?" I said. "I am freezing. I am not taking my shoes off."

"There are sticks, pine cones, and not to mention wild animals everywhere."

"What if I step on a porcupine?"

"A porcupine? Oh man, Frances!" Jaana said with a chuckle. "You know you really make me laugh, I forgot how funny you are."

"You forgot?" I said. "Have we met before?"

She ignored me and said, "Frances, they are more scared of you than you are of them."

"Famous last words," I mumbled to myself. "Hey, I'm from Baltimore! We don't do wild animals or nature."

Jaana looked right at me and said, "What does being from Baltimore have to do with anything about who you really are? You have existed long before Baltimore existed. Stop getting caught up in the character of Frances. Look past Frances; look to the one with no name."

Jaana bent down to remove her brown boots.

"So, the Nogos." Jaana's voice had turned serious. "They are kind of like Wolves"

"Okay… Wolves," I said out loud with a crack to my voice. "Are they shapeshifters? Like you?"

"No," Jaana said. "It is important to be very careful around them because they are a hundred percent animal and have animal instincts, which makes them hard to read."

"Okay. Well, if it gets too crazy, can't you shape-shift to protect us?" I asked.

"Yes and no," said Jaana. "Nogos are a lot bigger than my shape-shifting form of a wolf. They are three times my size. Our only defense would be to run. While Nogos are big and strong, they are slow. This is because they are only allowed to travel a couple of hundred feet from the portal they are protecting. If something goes wrong and I start running, promise me you will run too. Just follow me and run as fast as you can. Like your life depends on it, because in some ways it does."

Jaana grabbed my hand and looked me dead in the eyes with those eyes of hers that spoke many different languages, all of which I have no idea what they were saying. The only words I could make out were *trust me*.

"Do you promise, Frances?"

"Yes, I will try," I said in a soft voice. "But I am not as strong as you."

Jaana grabbed my hand and said, "It is not about the strength. It is not strength that moves the mountain, but the longing in a single fragile heart to see what is on the other side. Can you promise me one more thing?" she asked.

"What?"

"Take your shoes off. Believe me, you will thank me later."

I bent down and unlaced my shoes to take them off, slowly placing my bare feet on the ground. The warmth of my feet now throbbed against the cold of the prickly ground.

The path ahead of us looked like it went on forever. It was dark and the trees along the side grew together, creating a canopy that made the path look more like a tunnel adorned with what looked like thousand-year-old vines.

Jaana said, out of nowhere, as if reading my mind, "You know, some of these vines are thousands of years old, so intertwined you will never be able to find where one starts and the other ends. They will grow side by side until, well, who knows, until the end, if there is even an end."

Jaana continued, "It is beautiful they will be together, never separating, only becoming more a part of each other."

"Beautiful?" I said.

"Yes," Jaana said calmly.

"But they are just trees, do they even know the other exists?"

"Frances! Jaana said with certainty. "Yes! They are alive, they have consciousness. They are no different than you and me. no difference at all, Frances."

She said it sternly, as if disappointed I would ask such a question.

"There is one difference," I replied. "We do have to separate. I will be going home very soon."

With a slight smile and soft tone, Jaana said, "Yes and no. You will be going home soon, but we will be together always, Frances. Even when apart, we will be together."

This time, her smile was with her eyes and they were firm and knowing.

I had only known Jaana for a short time. However, she felt like a part of me; like a dear old friend I had been reunited with after a long absence. She had these expressions and mannerisms that I knew. Between her thoughts, sometimes she would put her hand to her mouth as if to catch a cough and gently clear her throat, then give a look of concentration. Other times, she would smile and her face looked like a 1000-piece puzzle I had put together myself, knowing each wrinkle dimple, and freckle intimately. All of these things made me feel like I had known her since creation. When she stood next to me in the dark, silent forest, her energy vibrated through the thin night air and hit my body, pulling me in the direction of her, always pulling me to her, and she too was pulled to me. The two pulls canceled each other out so the push and pull became a stillness. For a moment, there was no past and no future—only the moment of now did I experience when I was with her. I wondered if she felt this too. Maybe this was what everyone experienced here. I just knew I did not want to leave her side. I knew I would soon be home, back in Baltimore, and she would remain here. With that thought, my stomach ached.

She turned and looked at me for only a second and whispered in my ear, "Always. Never last long enough. So look to now. Now is always."

She picked up her pace and walked faster. She was now ahead of me, no longer beside me.

As we walked the path, it began to widen, and soon we were in an open field. Luckily the moon was full and it lit the path, and the grass shone a dark blue-green. I looked up directly at the moon. Its silver-blue light shone through, embracing me with warmth, and that was when I noticed my feet were no longer cold.

A mild breeze arrived and carried with it the smell of burning wood. It was sweet and arose my senses.

I started to hum a tune I didn't even know; it just came to me. There were no words to put to the humming and it relaxed me and I went into a waking daydream. The environment disappeared. Jaana was there, then she faded out, but I could feel her footsteps' vibrations beside me as I hummed and walked.

Jaana whispered, "You remember, don't you?"

"What? I said. "Remember what?"

"A humming blue," said Jaana.

Jaana began to tell a story, only it wasn't a story—it was an actual account of a past life we shared.

"We were brothers, Frances. Well, not blood brothers, but the best of friends. So close we were. We should have been brothers during that lifetime. I think we chose not to be because when we met in our early teens, we knew the connection was special. If we had been born in the same family, we would have thought our closeness was blood-bound, but our connection is soul-bound. You and I are soul-bound, Frances, and that lifetime is one of my favorites to remember.

"We met as young boys. We were only 14 years old, but in those days we were considered men. It was a different time. Older than our years. It was a time of violence and uncertainty. Each day was based on survival."

"That sounds familiar," I said under my breath.

"Frances, I know your life now is not easy, but always remember you picked that life and it is teaching you the things you need to progress in this life and future lives. Nothing is random or coincidental; everyone's life has a map, a path built into every single second lived. But let me get back to my story. As I said, it's my favorite," she said with a wide smile on her face.

"We were brought together by war. We lived in two different tribes. Our tribes came together as allies to fight a war. All of the young men were forced to fight."

"Wait, I was a boy in a past life?" I said, finally realizing what she was saying .

"Yes, you have been every sex, gender, and race on Earth. Everyone on Earth has been. That is why we choose Earth, because there are so many chances to play different roles. We met on the first day our villages gathered to talk of war. You were walking with your head down and walked right into me. You said, 'Excuse me' and you had tears in your eyes. I knew you were afraid."

"Afraid," I said. "I was afraid to fight, to get hurt?"

"No, Frances, you were afraid to kill, to be the one that would hurt another. I asked you your name, you said Hu, and with those words, I knew. Names are very important. They carry a vibration with them, a sound, a tone. A name is never an accident. Even if you are given the wrong name, the wrongness of the name can point you in the right direction. That can be said for a lot of things.

"From that first meeting, we were inseparable. We even slept together, shared a small hut made of sticks and mud. At night, the moonlight would cut through the misshapen branches, letting in the soft light and filling the room with a glow of what I could only call magic. When the nights were cold, we would lie together against each other for warmth. Some nights we would stay up late into the early morning, talking about our homes and our families. The man who commanded our group would come in often to yell at us because we would be carrying on and laughing while we were at war. But with you by my side, the war felt a thousand miles away, except when we were on the front line and death was staring us in the face.

"It was early in the morning on the day of the attack. The enemy tribe entered the camp very early. We were sitting in the light of dawn just before sunrise. The night fire was still slowly burning. I remember the burnt wood carried a sweetness on the wind. I heard the drums of war then the noise of a thousand men charging. The ground vibrated. It felt as if the Earth was splitting in two.

"We both jumped from our beds, our eyes open wide with fear. I grabbed you, Frances, and pushed you to the ground and said, 'Stay here. I will come back to you when it is safe.' You replied, 'No, Li.' Li was my name in that lifetime," Jaana said with a smile and a slant of her head. "Hu and LI," she whispered under her breath.

"You said to me, 'No, Li, I am a soldier. This is my fight too and I am not leaving your side.' I wasn't sure if you were a soldier or not but I was certain you would never leave my side. There was no use in trying to make you stay behind. 'Okay,' I said. 'Stay close.' You replied, 'I am going to stay so close you are going to think we are sewn together.' I laughed. Even in the middle of war, you could make me laugh. I thought it was a joke, but you were dead serious.

"We ran from the small hut and grabbed our swords. At first, it was hard to see which side was which. Our swords had a black sash on them. The enemy's sword, a red sash. I yelled, 'Hu, back-to-back,' and we both knew what to do. We had been trained that in tight combat, you should find a partner and put your backs together to create somewhat of a circle of protection so our backs would never be exposed to the enemy.

"We were doing so good, Frances. We moved in unison like magnets. I would pull one way to defend a blow and there you were, the backs of your heels hitting mine. I knew this was our best defense since we could read each other's mind.

"At some point, we were separated. A large man fell into you and knocked you over. You tried to recover. But he crushed you. Finally, you were able to recover but I had been pushed further down the field. The last thing I remember from that battle is a soldier with a red sash charging me. I was about to defend the charge. I had my sword up, ready, then you appeared in front of me. We were face to face, and you had a smile on your face, so happy that we were back together again, and then your face changed and I felt the sword from the man that was charging. He had impaled you all the way through and the tip rested in my side. As if we were sewn together. The sword and the needle held you to me. You took most of the brunt. He tried to pull the sword out. Your face twisted in agony. You screamed a scream I will never forget.

"I still had my sword in my hand. I held it high in the air. You grabbed my sword, reached it high over your own head, putting your hands behind the back of your head, and with all your might, you pushed the sword down and back. The sword entered the enemy's shoulder, coming out through his back. He fell to the ground, dead.

"All was still, and a coldness entered me. Your lips trembled, shaking with pain. Then blood bubbled out of your lips and nose. I could see you dying in front of me. Your eyes never closed, constantly looking into my eyes, and you had a slight smile as you let out the last exhale of breath. So close we were, I felt your last breath, hot and soft, brush against my cheek. That last breath was so rich with intent. I swear it was your soul reaching out to kiss me goodbye."

Jaana looked up with a tear in her eye and said, "That was my favorite of our lifetimes."

Jaana stopped. It looked like she was going to say more, but then a giant barking sound echoed through the forest. The sound was thunderous. I shook from the inside out, sending shivers down my back; vibrating all of my nerve endings. Jaana grabbed my arm and pulled me to the ground hard. She placed her ear to the cold ground. I did the same; I had no idea what she was doing but I wanted to make myself look useful.

"Nogos. I count three by the vibration they are making," Jaana said. "Look, there is a portal. See the blue light about 200 feet ahead?"

I said, "Well, no, not really, I only see three giant Nogos!"

"Yeah, if there was just one I could distract it and you could jump through the portal, but there are too many. We can't, this portal is too well guarded."

With that, all of a sudden a Nogo—the middle one, the biggest one—looked right at me and started charging.

Jaana whispered, "If I run then you run, Frances. Promise."

I swallowed a hard lump in my throat and said softly and with no sound, "Okay." But there must have been some sound because Jaana said, "Okay, let's do this!"

Then all three Nogos started to charge, their thick long fur stuttering, intent on attacking. Without so much as a pause, Jaana side-stepped and turned her back to the three of them, grabbing my hand once again. I was twirling in one motion. Now my back was to them as well.

"RUN!!!!" Jaana shouted. She pulled me forward again but then suddenly let my hand go, picking up her pace up to a speed I could not keep up with. She yelled, "Frances, catch me."

Just then, I was about to look back to see how close the Nogos were to us. Before I could turn my head, I heard Jaana yell, "Don't look back. Never look back. Catch me, Frances." With that, her speed increased again.

Jaana said, "I'm waiting for you."

With those words, my legs propelled forward, jerking my body with a painful shift, my torso swaying separate from the rest of my body.

My body started to vibrate the way a fast-moving locomotive would vibrate at capacity. My heart was pounding. I was sure my legs would separate from my body.

Then it happened.

"I transformed!" I yelled. That was the only way to describe it.

My clothes ripped from my body. With the speed of my running, they blew in the wind, falling to the side as I ran faster and faster. Thick fur started to grow from the pores of my once-smooth skin. I was running on all fours as if I were a dog. "A dog! I'm a dog?" I shouted out loud without knowing what I was saying. It was more a question than a statement.

Jaana yelled, "No, you are a wolf."

Then she howled. I looked up and saw that she too was a wolf and we were both running for our lives.

I howled as an involuntary response to her howl.

This was when I looked back and saw only an empty field. This was when I knew we would live.

Jaana, sensing my relief, looked back and said, "After we cross this river, we should be okay."

We approached the river. It was calm and the moon still lit everything with a silver glow. In the glow, the water became a mirror in which I could look at myself. My new self. I stood beside Jaana, looking into the water, seeing our reflection, except it was a reflection of myself I had never seen. Eyes an amber yellow staring back at me, solid black fur covering me, with only a small amount of white surrounding my mouth and jaw.

Jaana on the other hand was a white-gray wolf with the slightest of black around her mouth.

"They are gone," Jaana said to me. I looked at her, but no words were coming from her mouth.

"We lost them! I told you they are slow." Again, no words came from her mouth.

I finally tried to speak. "How am I hearing you right now?"

Instead of words, a series of muffled barks from the back of my throat came out.

Jaana, again with no words, said, "Just think about what you want to say. I will hear you."

I thought, "What just happened?!"

"We shifted. In this dimension, you will be able to shape-shift. However, I knew you would not know how to and didn't want to try to explain, because when you try to understand from intellect, that makes it harder to shift, especially for your first time. I knew the emotional rush from running would make you shift automatically. It came from your being, where the knowing of how to become is from."

"Okay, how do I shift back?"

Then a thud; my butt hit the soft, wet grass hard. I went to rub my butt and realized I was naked.

"I'm naked."

"I know," Jaana said with a giggle. "It's okay, I have seen you naked before. I have seen you naked in this body you call Frances and I have seen you naked as Hu. I have seen you in all lifetimes and in all forms. Forget the body. The body, your body, everyone's body is not real; it is only a protected tool with which to experience life. It is not real. What is real and eternal is you. The you without the name, without the body. The core of who you are is your consciousness, and consciousness has no form. It is only awareness with a choice between love and fear."

"How? What do you mean?" I said, a little afraid to hear the answer.

Jaana walked over, stood directly in front of me, placed her hand on my shoulders, looked me in the eyes, and said,

"I am you. You are me. I am your higher self, your eternal self. And you, you are my ego self. We are the same. The only difference is I know I am not a person. I am consciousness. I am a spiritual being. You, however, think you are a person in a body with the story of being Frances. Your whole identity is tied to those three facts. Person, body, Frances. I am consciousness. I have no form, so I am tied to nothing. I am free, Frances. Once you understand this and see it through my eyes, you will be free."

"Wait, can you explain in a different way? How are we standing in the same place at the same time if we are the same person?"

Jaana said, Time, place. What is that?" She leaned over and whispered in my ear, "A life is temporary, but an existence is forever. I am the existence."

Her eyes widened as she continued, "You, Frances, you are the life. You are a small piece of my consciousness in the form of a human body."

It was then I knew we were connected, a part of each other but also free of each other. Not in an earthly way; not the way a lover possesses the one they love. This was not about possession, but about unconditional love. A love without insecurity or jealousy because it came from the same source. There was no competition here. This love had been forged over thousands of lifetimes together, always returning to one another. One was the other's true north. I knew I was this to her and she was this to me. I did not have evidence; I didn't even have memories of it. I knew it in my being. The way my body knew how to shift from human to wolf to save my own life. She was in my DNA because we were the same. I understood what she meant when she said we were soul-bound.

"Frances, the love you saw coming from my eyes when we first met. Do you remember it?" she asked.

"I will never forget it," I said.

"That is because it was you looking at yourself. You saw and felt what it is like to love yourself unconditionally. It is a love unlike anything because it is truth in form. The truth of the Universe is not seen by everyone; it comes to those when they are ready, otherwise it can be very unnerving."

I said, "Why? Why would you separate yourself into two?

Jaana said, "For the same reason the source separated themself into a billion different pieces. Sometimes you have to make yourself very small in order to receive the greatest of teaching."

She smiled and said, "Let's find our clothes. I'm starting to get cold." Jaana walked close to me, picked up my hand, and squeezed it somewhat hard. "Imagine what you were wearing before, Frances. Every piece of clothing from your shirt to your shoes—don't forget your shoes. I know how much you like them," she said with a giggle, making fun of the fact that an hour ago I did not want to part with them and how now I stood naked to the world with nothing that I owned attached to me, not even my identity. I thought about that and knew that was real freedom.

I then imagined every piece of clothing I had on before the chase, and within a few seconds, we were both fully clothed again.

"How?" I said.

"In this place, intentions manifest instantly," Jaana said.

"What is this place?" I said with a small voice, not sure I wanted to know.

"Place," Jaana repeated. "Place is such a simple word to describe where we are, but maybe simplicity is the heart of truth and this place is truth. We are not in a physical place, but rather we are in a moment. A moment of teaching and understanding. This is a place in emptiness."

"Emptiness? Wait, how are we in emptiness? Look at all that is around us. I would not say it is empty."

Jaana said, "Look closer. Hold out your hand."

I held my hand out, and in the middle of my hand a green bud appeared and grew into a yellow rose. "What in the world?" I said.

Jaana said, "Once your hand was empty, but now it is full with the form of a yellow rose. In order for that rose to appear, there first had to be emptiness. Emptiness gives birth to form. The whole Universe, including Earth, came from emptiness. Emptiness has no limits because nothing defines it but emptiness. Some say emptiness is the same as nothing, but no, that is not true. Emptiness is the opposite of nothing; emptiness is everything. Anything with form is the child of emptiness. This place does not really exist. It is only an experience."

"Wait, what about the Nogos. We almost died? They were chasing us. That felt real to me—very real," I said.

"I know," Jaana said. "It felt as real as your life on Earth feels, but remember, that is not real either. Do you remember when you sat by the Inner Harbor in Baltimore and looked into the water and it changed into something beautiful, unpolluted, a paradise right before your eyes. That was possible because you saw it with your true nature which is love. Baltimore became a paradise within you and so it appeared outward. All outward appearances first begin inward. If everyone lived in love then the whole world would be a paradise.

The Nogos were part of the teaching; they were an illusion to help you create the desire to transform. Like I said, you needed motivation in order to shape-shift from human to wolf. If I asked you with words to do it, you would not have known how. I had to create a situation in order to motivate you to do it. It is the same on Earth. Your life is not real, but the teaching is real."

Jaana paused, then reiterated, "This world is the teaching. The world is exactly how it should be. If it was any other way, the teaching would be lost.

"Beings do not evolve to higher levels of consciousness without being motivated.

It takes many lives, many reincarnations to effectively be motivated enough to evolve."

I asked, "Motivated? What do you mean?"

"Yes, life gives a human being a multitude of choices, choices either based on fear or love. The more the human being picks a choice rooted in love, the more they evolve. Choices made on Earth have immediate consequences. These consequences motivate humans to learn from their mistakes. Hopefully, choosing love the next time around will make all the difference. When you make choices based on love for others, not just thinking of yourself, your life becomes easier because you are going with the divine plan of the Universe. You are living within the flow of the cosmic dream."

Jaana looked at me and smiled. Her smile was new; her eyes were new. I looked deep within her eyes, and for the first time, I saw my own self looking back at me. All the love was there like before, but now I recognized from whom that love came from. It was from me, my very own self.

She was right; all the desire and longing to have my mother love me was gone. It was as if the hole that had been inside me since birth disappeared. I continued to look into her eyes. It seemed like hours, but it must have only been a few minutes.

With just that look, years and lifetimes of insecurities, longing, and fear all dissolved. I only saw my own self holding me in love. Pouring love into me. Loving me as if I was deserving of love, as if I had never done anything wrong in my life, as if I had no shame, no guilt. The eyes were wise, soft, humble, funny, but most of all forgiving. They just loved me unconditionally.

"Frances, it is time for you to go now. "

"What do you mean? We still haven't found a portal to take me home," I said, worried.

Jaana said, "We never needed a portal; it was part of the teaching. It was part of the experience of this moment."

"Oh," I said, a little sad.

Jaana said, "I will hug you goodbye, and after the hug you will awake at home in your bed. You will wake as if from a deep sleep with no memory. You will say, 'I slept so well. I do not even remember my dreams.' One day, however, months or even years from now, you will sit down and start to write a story. The story will come because certain moments in your life will remind you that you have a story to tell. You will pick up a pencil and start to write this story. Once you write the story, you yourself will not know if it is a true story that really happened to you or if it is your imagination, and that is how it should be. It should remain uncertain until maybe one day it will be certain for you."

"Why?" I said.

"Because that is what life is: uncertain. And that is what allows it to continue—a surprise each and every day you open your eyes to the world."

It was then that Jaana winked at me and said, "Frances, it is time for you to go out into the world and surprise us."

9 798218 435165